A Carol

By

Alicia Lane Dutton

A Carolina Christmas
Copyright © 2017, Alicia Lane Dutton
All Rights Reserved

A CAROLINA CHRISTMAS (Christmas in Dixie at the time) received its world premiere at The Cumming Playhouse in Cumming, Georgia on November 29, 2018. It was directed by Al Dollar and Alicia Lane Dutton; choreography by Catherine Peets, Jace Haney, Misty Barber, and Al Dollar; set design by Alicia Lane Dutton and Edward Dutton; costume design by Alicia Lane Dutton; lighting design by Fallon Croxton and sound by David Harrell. The cast was as follows:

Ashley..Jessica Hill
Savannah.......................................Katherine Smith
Lance..Brian Slaton
Stephen...Jace Haney
Miss Margaret................................Gloria Wyatt
Dwayne...Al Dollar
Harley...Olivia Watts
Earline...Carmen Taylor
Ruby Sue...Tammi Scales
Bobby Lou..Nina Jones
Marla Jean......................................Lizzie Powers
Crawford.......................................Grier Friedman

My deepest gratitude.

Cast of Characters (8F) (4M)

Stephen: 20's, Marine, nice guy, from New Orleans

Lance: 20's, Marine, sarcastic, from Georgia

Savannah: 20's, sweet, pageant girl

Ashley: 20's, strong willed, pageant girl

Miss Margaret: 50's-70's, Proprietor of the new Lady Marmalade B & B

Dewayne: 30's-70's, Waffle Barn Manager/Cook

Harley: 20's-30's, Waffle Barn Waitress, confident

Earline: 40's-60's, seasoned Waffle Barn Waitress, former pageant queen

Ruby Sue: 40's-60's, pretentious, wealthy

Bobby Lou: 40's-60's, salt of the earth

Crawford: 20's-30's, young pastor

Marla Jean: 20's, very pregnant, would-be robber

A Carolina Christmas

(8F) (4M)

    A snowstorm has stranded Ashley and Savannah, two pageant queens, at the Spartanburg Airport. Having missed the Miss Toyland pageant in Atlanta, they will now have to enter Miss Chicken Plucker in order to win enough money to pay for the rest of graduate school. Two Marines, home on leave, are also stranded and the last available lodging anywhere near Spartanburg is a bed and breakfast in Bug Tussle, South Carolina. After its eccentric owner has waited more than a year, The Lady Marmalade Bed and Breakfast will finally have its first guests who throughout the course of their stay show that they aren't afraid of armored vehicles, hors d'oeuvres hours featuring Elvis robes, pregnant armed robbers at The Waffle Barn, and helping out The First Hope of The Last Chance Baptist Church with the threatened cancellation of its Food Pantry PaLooza.

A Carolina Christmas Song List

Pageant Queen
Rock a Bye Your Baby to a Dixie Melody
Under the Anheuser Busch
I Wonder Who's Kissing Her Now
Bring a Torch Jeanette Isabelle
Every Day is Ladies Day with Me
I Ain't Got Nobody
Way Down Yonder in New Orleans
There's a Little Bit of Bad in Every Good Girl
Jolly Old St. Nicholas
Toyland
O Holy Night
Go Tell It on the Mountain

ACT I
Scene 1

Spartanburg, South Carolina, Airport Terminal (Indicated with just a sign.) SAVANNAH and ASHLEY are wearing pageant gowns and they are each holding an overnight bag.

ASHLEY
I cannot believe this! That snow storm came out of no where! If the weatherman can't predict what's going to happen a few hours from now, how am I supposed to trust he's gonna know what the climate is in a hundred years?!
SAVANNAH
Don't start, Ashley! Right now we've got to figure out what we're gonna do. (Looks at phone) Our connecting flight into Atlanta has been officially canceled.
ASHLEY
We can rent a car! I'm not scared to drive in the snow! We'll get a big monster truck! Then we won't miss the pageant.
SAVANNAH
How many times do I have to tell you? It's not snow, it's ice. There's a difference.
ASHLEY
Surely someone has some way to get to Atlanta.
SAVANNAH
I think people just buy all the milk and bread they can carry and wait it out around here.
ASHLEY
I'm not waiting anywhere. I'm renting a truck and driving us to Atlanta.
SAVANNAH
I've already checked on that. All the roads have been officially closed. No one will rent a vehicle.
ASHLEY
I can't believe this! We don't even have any normal clothes with us and we're stranded in Alabama!
SAVANNAH
Listen! We did not have an extra seventy-five dollars to check a suitcase. Surely the airline will put us up somewhere for free.

And maybe they'll postpone the pageant.
ASHLEY
Let's hope. We're banking on that scholarship money.
(They exit.)

ACT 1
Scene 2

Spartanburg airport. LANCE and STEPHEN. They are carrying large duffel bags.

LANCE
We finally get granted Christmas leave and get stuck in South Carolina. Great.
STEPHEN
Why couldn't we have gotten stuck in Vegas or Miami? We could have at least spent Christmas in a strip club.
STEPHEN
Really?
LANCE
O.K. I'm kind of kidding, but not entirely.
STEPHEN
(Looks at his phone) Every hotel in Spartanburg is booked. The only thing that has an availability is something called The Lady Marmalade Bed and Breakfast. It says it's 23 miles from the airport in Bug Tussle, Alabama.
LANCE
That's clearly a no.
STEPHEN
The airline is putting us up for free. I'm not sleeping in the airport.
LANCE
I'm not sleeping in a place called Bug Tussle.
STEPHEN
Lots of places in the South have weird names. Come on. It might end up being cool. Right now my only requirement is food and a bed.
LANCE
That's a pretty low bar.
STEPHEN
It's a higher bar than we get in the Marines most of the time.
LANCE
True.

ACT 1
Scene 3

The Lady Marmalade Bed and Breakfast. A very modest dining room/living area with a sad small Christmas tree on the buffet. SAVANNAH and ASHLEY enter carrying their bags. They're shivering as they are still clad in their pageant gowns. MISS MARGARET enters bundled up in a coat, hat, and gloves.

SAVANNAH
I can't thank you enough for picking us up at the airport. I didn't know it was legal to own a tank.
MISS MARGARET
Yep. As long as you disable the gun. My late husband, Hubert, got a wild hair and bought it at an auction. I thought he was crazy, but it was fun to drive around on the farm and every blue moon when it snows it comes in handy.
ASHLEY
Clearly.
MISS MARGARET
Welcome to Lady Marmalade. You two are my first official guests.
SAVANNAH
Really? You've never had anybody here before?
MISS MARGARET
Nope. Y'all are like my guinea pigs I'll be testing on.
ASHLEY
(Flatly) Yay us. (to Savannah) We're gonna end up in a stew or something, like in Fried Green Tomatoes.
SAVANNAH
Cool it! Miss Margaret, we're gonna go up to our room and unpack.
ASHLEY
Unpack what? Our other two pageant outfits? Maybe you should ask her if she has a feed sack we could borrow or something.
MISS MARGARET
O.K. Sweetie. Y'all will be staying in the The King's Room.

SAVANNAH
Ooo! That sounds nice!
MISS MARGARET
Oh, it's my best room, for my very first guests!
ASHLEY
That actually sounds promising.
SAVANNAH
Thank you, Miss Margaret.
MISS MARGARET
You're welcome sweetheart.

SAVANNAH and ASHLEY exit. LANCE and STEPHEN enter carrying their large duffel bags. They are disheveled, out of breath, and appear sweaty.

STEPHEN
Hi Ma'am. Is this the Lady Marmalade Bed and Breakfast?
MISS MARGARET
It certainly is. How did you two get here? The state patrol closed the roads a few hours ago.
STEPHEN
We hitched a ride from the airport with a guy in a Jeep to Jasper.
LANCE
Then we ran the last ten miles.
MISS MARGARET
Oh my!
STEPHEN
We need a room. We have a voucher from the airline.
MISS MARGARET
Well, you're my second round of stranded guests tonight. I've already assigned The King's Room but I've still got The Blonde Bombshell room vacant.
LANCE
The Blonde Bombshell Room?
STEPHEN
See. Who needs Vegas?

MISS MARGARET
Ya'll will love it. Oh! Our themed wine and hors d'oeuvre nightcap party starts in half an hour. Your party robes are in your room on the back of the door. Where is my mind?! I forget to tell the girls!

MISS MARGARET exits.

LANCE
Girls? Party robes? Bug Tussle might not end up being so bad after all.

ACT 1
Scene 4

ASHLEY and SAVANNAH are holding a glass of wine. Each have on a white bathrobe decorated like Elvis' classic eagle costume. Their hoods are up which feature an Elvis wig tacked on. MISS MARGARET has on a robe decorated with feathers, sequins etc. with one of Patti Labelle's signature hairstyles adorning the hood.

SAVANNAH
Miss Margaret, who exactly was Lady Marmalade?
MISS MARGARET
Oh honey! The fabulous miss Patricia Louise! Otherwise known as Patti Labelle. Hubert and I would get our groove on back in the seventies (grinds and thrusts) to that song. I knew when I decided to open a bed and breakfast it had to be called The Lady Marmalade.
SAVANNAH
That's clever. We just normally say jelly at breakfast but marmalade sounds really sophisticated.
MISS MARGARET
I thought so too but the real reason I named the B and B Lady Marmalade was "voulez-vous coucher avec moi, ce soir?" (quote is sung)
ASHLEY
Excuse me?
MISS MARGARET
"Voulez-vous coucher avec moi, ce soir?" (again sung) It means, Do you want to sleep with me tonight? (She then sings loudly and soulfully) "Creole Lady Marmalade...."

LANCE and STEPHEN enter with their robes on with the hoods down. The robes are black with the classic white Marilyn Monroe Seven Year Itch dress design.

ASHLEY
Oh my.

MISS MARGARET
And here are our strapping Marines!
ASHLEY
Marines? Really?
MISS MARGARET
Ashley, Savannah, this is Lance and Stephen. Since y'all were already settled into The King's Room, I gave them the Blonde Bombshell Room. That room is my memorial to Hubert, God rest his soul. He had a real penchant for blondes and explosives.
LANCE
Yes, I thought the Marilyn posters and mine and grenade chachkies were lovely. By the way, those grenades and mines don't happen to be live do they?
MISS MARGARET
Oh, I don't think so!
STEPHEN
Just curious. How did you get your hands on so many grenades exactly?
MISS MARGARET
Hubert just loved to collect things that go boom! He got me didn't he! (She laughs loudly and does a pelvic thrust.)

LANCE and STEPHEN look quite horrified.

ASHLEY
So, Miss Margaret informed us that you don't get any refreshments unless you're fully costumed.
LANCE
Fully costumed?
MISS MARGARET
Oh yes, Lance! This is Lady Marmalade's first official nightcap party and everyone has to be dressed appropriately. Hoods please!

LANCE and STEPHEN reluctantly put on their hoods revealing Marilyn wigs tacked to the top.

ASHLEY
Nice.
LANCE
Now, can I please have a beer?

ACT 1
Scene 5

LANCE, STEPHEN, ASHLEY, and SAVANNAH still have on their robes, but their hoods are all down. LANCE and STEPHEN both have beers and ASHLEY and SAVANNAH are both drinking wine. They are all clearly inebriated.

SAVANNAH
I still can't believe y'all ran here.
ASHLEY
I don't run unless someone has a gun pointed at me.
STEPHEN
Does that happen very often?
ASHLEY
Only occasionally.
LANCE
I can't believe you rode to the Lady Marmalade in a tank.
STEPHEN
I can't believe Miss Margaret can drive a tank.
SAVANNAH
I have to admit the woman is full of surprises.

LANCE flips up the hood on his robe.

LANCE
You think?
ASHLEY
I can't believe nobody here will drive in the snow.
SAVANNAH, STEPHEN
It's ice. It's different.

SAVANNAH and STEPHEN give one another a surprised look as if they are kindred spirits.

LANCE
Well Ashley, I can't believe that girls prance around on a stage in dresses for a crown.

SAVANNAH
Uh oh.
ASHLEY
I could see how you would feel that way except that it's hard to take a man seriously who's dressed as Marilyn Monroe.

LANCE flips his hood down.

SAVANNAH
Listen. A lot of people think that's the way all pageants are but it's a lot more than that.
LANCE
Really?
ASHLEY
Yes, really.
SAVANNAH
Ashley and I met in college. She was Miss Junior Miss of Texas and I was Miss Junior Miss of Mississippi. (She takes a swig of wine from the bottle.) I still love saying that. Miss Mississippi! Miss Mississippi!
ASHLEY
She's very passionate about pageants.
SAVANNAH
You are too little missy and don't try to deny it. We got a full ride through college with our Junior Miss winnings.
LANCE
You're kidding.
ASHLEY
She's not. We got free tuition, dorm, books, and a meal ticket.
LANCE
And to think I joined the Marines and laid it on the line for the G.I. Bill and all I really had to do was..(He stands and pulls apart the robe a little and exposes his extended leg.)
SAVANNAH
Woo Hoo!! (She takes another swig.)
ASHLEY
There's just a little more to it than that. But I must say I'm impressed. Your legs are a lot more feminine than I would have thought.

LANCE
Very funny.
SAVANNAH
We've been wanting to go to graduate school, so we developed a strategy to pay for it.
ASHLEY
I am a pageant strategist! IF that was a thing!
SAVANNAH
Ashley found all the pageants we hadn't aged out of.
ASHLEY
Not a word from you two!
SAVANNAH
We enter them and no matter which of us wins or places, we pool our money for graduate school. We're one pageant away from completing our goal!
STEPHEN
You're kidding! That's great.
SAVANNAH
It WAS great until we got stranded in Bug Tussle, South Carolina. (She says South Carolina through a long wail.)
STEPHEN
I'm sure there'll be another pageant somewhere soon.
LANCE
Which pageant are y'all missing?
ASHLEY
Not important!
SAVANNAH
The-
ASHLEY
Irrelevant!
SAVANNAH
The Miss-
ASHLEY
Fake news!
SAVANNAH
The Miss Toyland Pageant!
LANCE
Reeallly!!

SAVANNAH
Yeeeessss! (Takes a swig of wine from the bottle.)
LANCE
Miss Toyland! Sounds like a place I'd like to go.
STEPHEN
Lance!
ASHLEY
He's right. It sounds stupid. It's just that if we could place or win, we would have graduate school completely paid for.
SAVANNAH
No loans, no debt. (She takes another swig.) And the pageant would have been fun too.

SAVANNAH

PAGEANT QUEEN

I'VE BEEN IN PAGEANTS SINCE I'S IN THE WOMB
MOM WAS PREGNANT AND WON MISS DOGWOOD
BLOOM I HAVE A CLOSET OF SEQUINED GOWNS
AND SHALLOW THOUGHTS BENEATH MY RHINESTONE
CROWN BUT I DON'T CARE WHAT THE PEOPLE SAY
I'VE GOT A SHERRI HILL DRESS AND HEELS THAT SLAY
CHORUS
I WAS BORN TO BE A PAGEANT QUEEN
MISS PIG JIG, MISS CRAWDAD, MISS COTTON PICKIN
QUEEN
I DUCT TAPE MY BOOBS AND I VASELINE MY TEETH I
KEEP MY SOCIAL MEDIA NON OBSCENE
NO SEX OR DRUGS I AM SQUEAKY CLEAN
SWIMSUIT COMPETITION MAKES ME A WORKOUT
FIEND I WIN CROWNS, AND TROPHIES, AND
SCHOLARSHIPS AND JUST LAST WEEK I WON MISS
SHRIMP AND GRITS OF THE CAROLINA COAST
AND VERY SOON I'LL BE MISS ALABAMA GOAL POST
SOME PAGEANTS MAKE YOU HAVE A TALENT
SOME GIRLS HAVE THEM BUT OTHERS HAVEN'T SOME
TWIRL BATONS AND DO ACROBATICS

THERE'S TAP DANCING, SINGING AND BAD DRAMATICS
MY FRIEND GRACE DID WHAT SHE WAS ABLE
HER MOMMA WAS A WAITRESS SO SHE SET A TABLE
CHORUS
I WAS BORN TO BE A PAGEANT QUEEN
MISS PIG JIG, MISS CRAWDAD, MISS COTTON PICKIN QUEEN
I DUCT TAPE MY BOOBS AND I VASELINE MY TEETH
I KEEP MY SOCIAL MEDIA NON OBSCENE NO SEX OR DRUGS I AM SQUEAKY CLEAN
SWIMSUIT COMPETITION MAKES ME A WORKOUT FIEND I WIN CROWNS, TROPHIES, AND SCHOLARSHIPS
BIG CASH PRIZES AND DON'T YOU KNOW
COLLEGE IS PAID FOR, AND ALMOST GRADUATE SCHOOL SAVANNAH'S MOMMA DIDN'T RAISE NO FOOL
AH HA HA HA AH HAA......

ACT 1
Scene 6

The next morning. STEPHEN, LANCE, SAVANNAH, and ASHLEY are sitting at the breakfast table still in their party robes clearly hung over. MISS MARGARET enters the room carrying a small boom box. There are several full mason jars, and loaves of bread in its packaging on the table. There are also two gallons of milk.

MISS MARGARET
Well good morning, everyone! (said loudly and in a sing song manner as to cause pain to those hungover) The party robes are only required for the nightcap party. Y'all could have worn any ole thing this morning.
SAVANNAH
These are super comfortable. Plus, we only have our pageant clothes with us.
LANCE
This is getting better and better.
ASHLEY
It cost seventy-five dollars to check a bag and we were just going to fly to Atlanta long enough to participate in that pageant and then get back to Houston. We didn't count on all this.
MISS MARGARET
You know my Hubert always said, be prepared!
STEPHEN
Oo rah!
MISS MARGARET
There's only one way to truly start the morning here at The Lady Marmalade. I'll need everyone to stand please.

Slowly everyone gets to their feet, holding their head, pressing on their temples etc. MISS MARGARET places the boom box on the table and presses a button. The Star Spangled Banner begins to play very loudly. Everyone reacts groaning, squinting their eyes, dropping their heads, etc. ASHLEY and

SAVANNAH have their hands over their hearts and LANCE and STEPHEN are saluting. ASHLEY yells over the music.

ASHLEY
I'm starving!

MISS MARGARET turns off the music.

MISS MARGARET
Well, we can finish the anthem later. You know, it actually has four stanzas instead of just the one everyone's familiar with.
LANCE
Oh goody!
MISS MARGARET
It's my first official breakfast at The Lady Marmalade and although the snowstorm threw me for a little loop I'm still prepared.
STEPHEN
Yes! Bring on the grease.
MISS MARGARET
Well, I don't know about that but I of course have all the milk and bread you could ever want. And my canning pantry has saved the day.
ASHLEY
Canning pantry?
SAVANNAH
My grandmother used to can! She always warned us about the pressure cooker exploding and blowing us all to smithereens! I was too scared to learn to can after that.
MISS MARGARET
It's a lost art. Instead of letting that snow storm get the best of us, we have food for days! (She lifts up the first jar.) This is my famous canned fig cucumber jelly.

STEPHEN heaves a little into his napkin. Everyone is mortified.

LANCE
In the same can?

MISS MARGARET
No silly!
SAVANNAH
Thank goodness.
MISS MARGARET
The same jar! I don't know why they call it canning when the magic happens in a mason jar.
ASHLEY
Fig and cucumbers. It sounds very gourmet but I'm just a simple grape jelly girl myself.
MISS MARGARET
Thank you honey! But ever since they started plopping figs on top of steaks and everything else in fancy restaurants, I figured I could get on the gourmet bandwagon too. I've got a fig tree out back and I've got about all I can eat even after the worms get theirs.

STEPHEN quickly exits heaving.

LANCE
So, Miss Margaret, I see lots of jars. What are some of our other choices? Anything a little less gourmet?
MISS MARGARET
Oh yes. Here's one of Hubert's favorites. Squash and honey dew melon jelly. The yellow and green mix kind of makes it look like goose poop, so Hubert nicknamed it Goose Poop Jelly. Oh, and this was my mother's famous recipe, cantaloupe bell pepper butter jelly. She won four state fair blue ribbons with that jelly.
ASHLEY
Really? That's surprising.
MISS MARGARET
Yes indeed. Well, I'm not sure if it was technically the state fair but it was the biggest fair in Armenia. Momma was Armenian.

STEPHEN enters wiping his mouth.

LANCE
Miss Margaret here was just telling us about her mother's

famous (slowly, playfully) cantaloupe bell pepper butter jelly. Here's you a nice helping to go with all that bread and milk.

LANCE spoons some onto Stephen's plate. STEPHEN quickly exits again.

MISS MARGARET
Well, I'm gonna leave y'all to it. I've got to get back to the canning pantry and pick out what we're gonna have for our hors d' oeuvres social hour tonight.

MISS MARGARET exits.

SAVANNAH
I was going to try so hard to make lemonade from the lemons we got handed here at Christmas, but instead, we ended up with goose poop jelly.
ASHLEY
I feel like I'm going to faint. I need some calories.
LANCE
Look, Stephen and I saw a Waffle Barn while we were running here. It's only about four miles up the road. They hardly ever close. Maybe Miss Margaret will let us borrow the tank.
SAVANNAH
I don't want to hurt her feelings!
ASHLEY
Count me in. I'm getting to that Waffle Barn if it's the last thing I do.
SAVANNAH
Someone needs to eat some of this!

LANCE and ASHLEY look at SAVANNAH. SAVANNAH looks around. She starts spooning the contents of one of the jars into the centerpiece.

ACT 1
Scene 7

The Waffle Barn. A classic diner with a counter, booths, and a door to a restroom. DEWAYNE can be seen through the pass through window. EARLINE is wiping down a table. HARLEY is clearing the dishes in front of RUBY SUE at the counter. STEPHEN, LANCE, ASHLEY, and SAVANNAH enter. ASHLEY and SAVANNAH have on their costumes for the Christmas sportswear division (example snowman, Christmas tree dress, leg lamp dress, etc.)

EARLINE
Welcome to the Waffle Barn! Y'all must really want some waffles coming through all that snow.
LANCE
More than you can imagine.
SAVANNAH
It wasn't too bad since we borrowed Miss Margaret's tank.
DEWAYNE
Correction, Hubert's tank.
EARLINE
Well he couldn't take it to heaven with him so it's officially Margaret's tank.
DEWAYNE
Whatever.
EARLINE
Ignore him. Y'all have a seat anywhere you'd like. And my goodness aren't WE in the Christmas Spirit.
ASHLEY
(Making it up) We're going to a... costume party later.
HARLEY
A Christmas costume party? I guess people are taking those ugly sweater parties to the next level.

STEPHEN, LANCE, SAVANNAH, and ASHLEY have a seat.

RUBY SUE
It looks like Margaret finally got her first guests at The Lady Marmalade Bed and Breakfast. And it took a blizzard to do it.
ASHLEY
How long exactly has The Lady Marmalade been open for business?
RUBY SUE
About a year. She opened it six months after Hubert died.
SAVANNAH
She must have gotten so lonely.
RUBY SUE
Not a lot of folks come through Bug Tussle I'm afraid.

RUBY SUE exits.

SAVANNAH
I feel so guilty now. I should have just stayed and eaten the goose poop.
HARLEY
Excuse me?
SAVANNAH
Never mind.

STEPHEN picks up a menu and looks at it.

STEPHEN
We'll take Miss Margaret some carry out. We'll get her this special, "The Whole Kit and Kaboodle." Two waffles, hash browns, eggs, bacon, ham, sausage, and country gravy.
ASHLEY
It sounds like you're trying to kill her.
LANCE
She'll have choices. It's not like we know her tastes except for random combination jellies.
SAVANNAH
Marmalades.
LANCE
Whatever.

SAVANNAH
O.K. that makes me feel better.

EARLINE approaches the table.

EARLINE
My name is Earline. How can I help you good folks?
LANCE
We'll take lots of caffeine and grease.
EARLINE
Ah huh. Sounds like y'all have a case of the after effects.
STEPHEN
I'm afraid you're right.
EARLINE
How about four Hangover Helper Platters, cokes, and coffee.
STEPHEN, LANCE, ASHLEY, SAVANNAH
Yes!
LANCE
While we're waiting, I would love to hear more about The Miss Toyland Pageant.
ASHLEY
No. If I thought you were truly interested, I'd oblige you, but you really just want to taunt us.
LANCE
Not true. If all I wanted to do was taunt you, I have plenty of fodder for that with just that getup you have on.
STEPHEN
I think they're kind of sexy.
SAVANNAH
Ooo. Thank you. You know, Ashley, maybe Lance is sincerely interested. We could educate him a little about these crazy pageants.
LANCE
Oh yes, please enlighten me.
SAVANNAH
The very best thing about pageants is that I met Ashley at a pageant and we've been best friends ever since.

ASHLEY
Thank you. It's true. You meet people. Some people you end up hating and some people you actually end up being friends with for life. And, of course, the main reason to do it is money for college.
LANCE
As previously said by every stripper in America.
ASHLEY
Has it ever occurred to you that at least a few of those strippers might be telling the truth?
LANCE
No.
SAVANNAH
You know, it's not easy. Some people could never get up in front of a big audience and answer difficult interview questions and-
STEPHEN
What kind of questions?
SAVANNAH
Crazy questions with sometimes impossible answers! You have to really channel your inner politician.
EARLINE
Here's y'all some drinks. I couldn't help hearing you talk about pageants which really explains a lot about your choice of attire. I used to be in pageants when I was young.
SAVANNAH
Really?
EARLINE
Yep. Some of the best memories of my life. I'm the former Miss East Bug Tussle Fair Queen.
LANCE
They actually divided the fairs into East and West Bug Tussle?
EARLINE
Yeah. I'm afraid so. They had a big rift because of a disagreement in the hog judging protocol. So some of the folks splintered off. The only real difference is that now we have the fair for two weeks instead of one. They flip a coin every year to see who gets the first week. There's always two different Fair Queens but they have to share the Christmas float.

LANCE
Fascinating.
EARLINE
They handled it pretty well though. The Fair Queen float was the first float in the parade so when it came to the end of the parade route, the driver would speed that sucker back to the end of the line and Miss East and West Bug Tussle would trade sides and they'd start the parade route over. You know, so the spectators could get a good look at both queens.
SAVANNAH
Did the fair queen pageant have a talent division, Earline?
EARLINE
Oh yes, honey. That was back before these hotel conference room pageants with the fake teeth and hair. We were the real thing! (pokes out her breasts)
ASHLEY
What did you do for your talent Earline?
EARLINE
I sang my favorite song.
SAVANNAH
Let's hear it!
EARLINE
Do you mind Dewayne?
DEWAYNE
I've got four Hangover Helper Platters and a Whole Kit and Kaboodle to make so it's gonna take a while. Have at it.

HARLEY grabs a (spatula, rolling pin etc.) to hand to EARLINE to use as a pretend microphone.

EARLINE

ROCK A BYE YOUR BABY TO A DIXIE MELODY

ROCK-A-BYE YOUR BABY TO A DIXIE MELODY
WHEN YOU CROON, CROON A TUNE FROM THE HEART OF DIXIE
JUST HANG THAT CRADLE, MAMMY MINE RIGHT ON THAT MASON-DIXON LINE

AND SWING IT FROM VIRGINIA TO TENNESSEE WITH
ALL THE LOVE THAT'S IN YA
"WEEP NO MORE, MY LADY" - SING THAT SONG AGAIN,
FOR ME
SING SOFT AND LOW JUST AS THOUGH YOU HAD ME ON
YOUR KNEE
A MILLION BABY KISSES, I'LL DELIVER
IF YOU WILL ONLY SING THAT "SWANEE RIVER"
ROCK-A-BYE YOUR ROCK-A-BYE BABY TO A DIXIE
MELODY "WEEP NO MORE, MY LADY" - SING THAT SONG
AGAIN, FOR ME
SING SOFT AND LOW JUST AS THOUGH YOU HAD ME ON
YOUR KNEE
A MILLION BABY KISSES, I'LL DELIVER
IF YOU WILL ONLY SING THAT "SWANEE RIVER"
ROCK-A-BYE YOUR ROCK-A-BYE BABY TO A DIXIE
MELODY

SAVANNAH
That was great!!!
HARLEY
You should do that every day! No telling what kind of tips it would get ya!
EARLINE
Thanks Harley but that was just one blast from the past. I don't think I'll be making it a habit.
LANCE
Well maybe you should consider it. She's right. There's a diner in New York where all the waiters and waitresses sing and it's always packed. You could become the biggest attraction in Bug Tussle.
EARLINE
That's mighty nice of you to say. I'll think about it.

ACT 1
Scene 8

Waffle Barn. SAVANNAH, ASHLEY, LANCE, STEPHEN, and HARLEY are present. The table is full of empty plates and crumpled napkins.

ASHLEY
I feel so much better.
STEPHEN
The Hangover Helper Platter lives up to its name.
HARLEY
Y'all might be in Bug Tussle longer than you thought. It's snowing again and they say it won't get above freezing for a while.
STEPHEN
We're used to being away from home for the holidays. I just feel bad for you ladies.
ASHLEY
I don't mind that so much as missing the pageant and the opportunity to make the last bit of money we needed to pay for school.
LANCE
Wasn't there a chance neither of y'all would win Miss Toyland?
ASHLEY
Of course, but I was desperately hoping that wouldn't happen.
SAVANNAH
Ashley just didn't want to have to go to our next competition if we didn't win Miss Toyland.
STEPHEN
What's the next competition?
ASHLEY
Don't say it.
SAVANNAH
Miss-
ASHLEY
More fake news.

SAVANNAH
Chicken Plucker.
LANCE
Miss Chicken Plucker?
ASHLEY
You had to say it.
SAVANNAH
Miss Chicken Plucker is kind of a big deal. A national poultry company sponsors it. Besides the ten thousand dollars in prize money, you get free eggs for life. We figured between the money for tuition and all the omelettes we could eat during graduate school, we'd be set. That was the only reason Ashley agreed to it.
LANCE
Ten thousand dollars?!!! Are you kidding?
SAVANNAH
Well, it's kind of like buying a lottery ticket with much better odds. We still have to pay an entry fee and have our evening gowns and outfits, especially for the themed pageants but Ashley can sew so that helps.
STEPHEN
You can sew? My mother could sew. She made me wear ridiculous knickers in fabric that matched my sister's dresses until I yanked a pair off on the church playground one day and told her I wouldn't be wearing knickers anymore. I figured my chances of not getting bullied were better in my Ninja Turtle Underoos.
LANCE
Wow, sewing is a lost art. I'm impressed.
ASHLEY
Thanks. I hope you're as impressed tomorrow when Savannah is waltzing around in her sugar plum fairy costume and I'm channeling my inner nutcracker.
LANCE
Oo! Nutcracker?
SAVANNAH
Yes. Our production number costumes are the last outfits we have with us.

LANCE
Tomorrow can't get here soon enough.
STEPHEN
What about the day after that? I doubt Miss Margaret and you ladies share the same style.
SAVANNAH
Well, we only had our pageant gowns on a couple of hours so looks like we'll be pretty gussied up for Christmas Eve.
STEPHEN
I think you ladies are pretty brave getting up on that stage in front of all those people… judging you.
ASHLEY
I figure people judge you every day on some level. Savannah and I might as well be making money to pay for school getting judged.
LANCE
So did the Miss Toyland pageant have a talent competition or was it going to be one of those beauty only pageants with bikinis?
ASHLEY
I don't do those kinds of pageants. It has to have at least a little substance, especially if I'm going to have to do a production number costumed as a southern belle, a catfish, or as in this case, a nutcracker.
STEPHEN
You had to dress up as a catfish?
SAVANNAH
Not exactly. We just had to wear these catfish tails for the opening number.
LANCE
Priceless. I want to see a picture.
ASHLEY
Careful now. I won two thousand dollars and the coveted title of Coosa County Catfish Queen.
LANCE
And to think I won Mr. Greek Week and got nothing but a new beer funnel.
SAVANNAH
What was Mr. Greek Week?

LANCE
A charity fundraiser for our fraternity in college.
ASHLEY
Did you have to have a talent or was it only about the oiled down pecs and spray tan?
LANCE
You did have to have a talent, actually.
STEPHEN
I've managed to serve two tours in Afghanistan with you and funny how this has never come up.
LANCE
Pageant talk isn't usually on the top of the agenda when you're killing terrorists.
STEPHEN
Do elaborate, won't you?
LANCE
That's all there is to it. I represented my fraternity, raised a lot of money for Habitat for Humanity, and got my shiny new beer funnel. End of story.
ASHLEY
I want to see your talent.
LANCE
Oh honey, there'll be plenty of time for that later. We're gonna be snowed in for a while.
ASHLEY
Very funny.
SAVANNNAH
No really! Let me guess…you juggled, you did stand-up comedy…you're a ventroliquist.
STEPHEN
I bet he sang. He never shuts up. He sings in the shower, on the shooting range, and he sang Christmas carols the whole time we were running to the Lady Marmalade in the snow.
LANCE
You're welcome.
ASHLEY
I want to hear it. I want to hear what helped you win Mr. Greek Week. Are you scared Marine?

STEPHEN
Uh oh. She's good.
SAVANNAH
You have no idea.
LANCE
I'm not scared.
ASHLEY
Then what are you waiting for?

LANCE nervously stands and clears his throat and does a few funny vocal exercises.

STEPHEN
Come on already!

LANCE

UNDER THE ANHEUSER BUSCH

TALK ABOUT THE SHADE OF THE SHELTERING PALMS
PRAISE THE BAMBOO TREE AND ITS WIDE SPREADING CHARMS
THERE'S A LITTLE BUSH THAT GROWS RIGHT HERE IN TOWN
YOU KNOW ITS NAME IT HAS WON SUCH RENOWN
OFTEN WITH MY SWEETHEART JUST AFTER THE PLAY
TO THIS LITTLE PLACE THEN MY FOOTSTEPS WILL
STRAY IF SHE HESITATES WHEN SHE LOOKS AT THE
SIGN SOFTLY I WHISPER, "NOW SUE, DON'T DECLINE...."
COME, COME, COME AND MAKE EYES WITH ME UNDER THE ANHEUSER BUSH
COME, COME DRINK SOME BUDWEISER WITH ME UNDER THE ANHEUSER BUSH
HEAR THE OLD GERMAN BAND
JUST LET ME HOLD YOUR HAND - YAH!
DO, DO COME AND HAVE A STEIN OR TWO UNDER THE ANHEUSER BUSH!

(LANCE PUTS HIS HAND OUT TO ASK ASHLEY TO WALTZ)

COME, COME, COME AND MAKE EYES WITH ME UNDER THE ANHEUSER BUSH
COME COME DRINK SOME BUDWISER WITH ME UNDER THE ANHEUSER BUSH
HEAR THE OLD GERMAN BAND
JUST LET ME HOLD YOUR HAND YAH!
DO, DO COME AND HAVE A STEIN OR TWO UNDER THE ANHEUSER BUSH!

ACT 1
Scene 9

SAMANTHA, ASHLEY, LANCE, and STEPHEN enter The Lady Marmalade. SAVANNAH is holding a to go box.

MARGARET
Welcome back!
SAVANNAH
We brought you a Whole Kit and Kaboodle from the Waffle Barn just in case you were hungry.
MARGARET
How thoughtful! How was the tank ride?
STEPHEN
Miss Margaret, do you know how many people you could get to come to stay at The Lady Marmalade if they thought it included a complimentary tank ride?
MARGARET
Not really.
STEPHEN
There are old veterans-
LANCE
And young veterans
STEPHEN
And young veterans who would love to come to this place.
MARGARET
I never really thought about that.
STEPHEN
We're all going to leave you a review on Holler and Trip Advice. And I'll bet you you'll have more guests than you can shake a stick at.
MARGARET
You think? I don't know.
ASHLEY
It's true Miss Margaret. You just need some reviews and people talking about how wonderful The Lady Marmalade really is.

SAVANNAH
Let's go take some pictures! Everything is so beautiful covered in snow! Even the tank!
STEPHEN
Good idea!

STEPHEN and SAVANNAH exit.

MARGARET
Oh my! I haven't pulled the ingredients for the hors d' oeuvres social hour this afternoon. It's gonna have a Christmas twist!
ASHLEY
Pulled the ingredients from where may I ask?
MARGARET
The canning pantry of course! With all the choices in there it might take a while, but I'm thinking of cattail pickles and sauerkraut with a hint of ground candy cane.
LANCE
Miss Margaret, how much food do you have in the canning pantry?
MARGARET
Well, I'm not exactly sure how much is in the pantry, but I have a root cellar with about a thousand mason jars full of canned deliciousness when the pantry runs dry.
LANCE
Did you and Mr. Hubert happen to be preppers?
MARGARET
Preppers? Oh no honey, those people are strange! Well, gotta get to my hostessing duties!(Exits.)
LANCE
She's something else.
ASHLEY
She is indeed.
LANCE
I'm really sorry you're missing your pageant.
ASHLEY
It's O.K. But I was really hoping to avoid Miss Chicken Plucker.

LANCE
So, what are you guys going to graduate school for?
ASHLEY
Education. We're teachers.
LANCE
That's noble. When you graduate, I'll have to start addressing you as professor.
ASHLEY
I won't be a professor. I'm getting my master's degree so I can go to India and teach.
LANCE
India?
ASHLEY
I went on a mission trip there and fell in love with the place. The people were so poor but their lives were still full of joy.
LANCE
The Marines have sent me to a lot of places like that.
ASHLEY
I guess it's kind of the "teach a man to fish" thing. If I can help instruct other people how to be teachers and they go out and start teaching then everybody wins.
LANCE
You know I also wanted to tell you I'm sorry you're stuck in Bug Tussle for Christmas.
ASHLEY
You too. I'm sure you don't get a lot of Christmases off.
LANCE
True, but I'm kind of used to it.
ASHLEY
You know, I had actually dreaded Christmas this year, but it might not turn out so bad.

STEPHEN and SAVANNAH enter.

STEPHEN
We got some good pictures.
SAVANNAH
Let's get to writing some reviews.

STEPHEN holds up his phone.

STEPHEN
I've already written mine. The Lady Marmalade Bed and Breakfast in the laid-back town of Bug Tussle, South Carolina, is the perfect getaway for retired military folks who appreciate good food, good company, and armored vehicles!

ACT 1
Scene 10

LANCE, STEPHEN, and SAVANNAH are lounging around The Lady Marmalade.

LANCE
That Ashley is a tough cookie. I was surprised when she said she was going out to gather Magnolia leaves (pine branches etc.) to make Miss Margaret a Christmas wreath.

SAVANNAH
Don't let her fool you. That girl's got a heart of gold. She's just been different since the incident.

STEPHEN
The incident?

LANCE
Do tell.

SAVANNAH
Well, it's probably one reason why she isn't too torn up about not being home for Christmas. Last Christmas she was supposed to get married but apparently the groom had other plans.

LANCE
Other plans?

SAVANNAH
Yes, other plans. Like he evidently planned to sleep with one of Ashley's bridesmaids after the rehearsal dinner.

STEPHEN
That's a bad plan.

SAVANNAH
Well, when Ashley found out, he told her he was sorry and just felt like he needed to sow some wild oats before they got married.

LANCE
Sowing his oats to her bridesmaid the night before their wedding? Definitely not the best plan.

SAVANNAH
Tell me about it. Ashley was in shock and so brokenhearted. But she put on her big girl panties and got them both back.

LANCE
I can only imagine.
SAVANNAH
She waited right up 'til the preacher asked if there was anyone who thought the wedding shouldn't go on to speak or forever hold their peace.
LANCE
And she doesn't seem like a girl who holds her peace a lot. At least upon first impressions.
SAVANNAH
She said, well since Sissy and Dylan were apparently sowing their wild oats all over each other last night, I'm gonna have to say that maybe I shouldn't become Mrs. Dylan Sumners. And Since my name would be Ashley Strickland Sumners, I've realized what my monogram would be and marrying you would definitely make me an A-S-S. So here he is Sissy! Since y'all decided to consummate your love to one another last night you can have him! And she slammed her bouquet in Sissy's hands and left.
STEPHEN
Did Sissy marry Dylan?
SAVANNAH
Oh heavens no. She was engaged to Logan Brightwell, one of Dylan's groomsmen and needless to say Logan called off their engagement right then and there.
LANCE
Ouch.
SAVANNAH
Yeah, so I kind of think she's happy we got stranded here and she won't have to go home for Christmas even though now we've got to do the Miss Chicken Plucker pageant.
STEPHEN
Well, what about you? Aren't you upset you're missing Christmas with your family?
SAVANNAH
I mean, of course. I figured I'd have Miss Toyland behind me and be helping my Mom cook turkey and dressing and sweet potato pie. But the weather had different plans. I can't change anything, so I just want to make the best of it.

ASHLEY enters holding a bag full of Magnolia leaves(etc.)
She's uncharacteristically bubbly.

ASHLEY
I got all the leaves (branches, etc.) for the wreath. After I make it, I'm going to make a garland for the fireplace. The Lady Marmalade will be pretty as a picture for Christmas.
SAVANNAH
I'll go get more leaves (branches, etc.) for the garland.
ASHLEY
Oh, get some pine cones too. (She gives Stephen the eye.)
STEPHEN
I'll help you.

STEPHEN and SAVANNAH exit.

LANCE
That's really sweet of you to help Miss Margaret decorate the place.
ASHLEY
Well, I figured we could take pictures of it all decked out for Christmas. It'll make the web page I'm making for her look really nice.
LANCE
You don't seem exactly sad to be stuck here in Bug Tussle for Christmas.
ASHLEY
I mean, there are worse places to be stuck, right?
LANCE
Like at home? Savannah told us what happened last Christmas.
ASHLEY
Water under the bridge. But I'd be lying if I didn't say I was relieved I'm here and not back in Abilene.
LANCE
Is the former groom still around?

ASHLEY
Afraid so. Needless to say, I've tried to avoid Abilene like the plague for the past year.
LANCE
What exactly does one do after they leave the groom at the altar? Just curious.
ASHLEY
After I stormed out of the wedding, Savannah threw my bags in her car and we were like Thelma and Louise cruising down the interstate in a bridesmaid dress and wedding gown. We went on my honeymoon and partied our tails off....on Dylan's dime of course.
LANCE
Then what happened?
ASHLEY
For a few months he begged me to elope. Told me he'd made a huge mistake. But I moved in with Savannah and then we decided to start entering pageants again to pay for graduate school. We start next fall.
LANCE
Do you ever wonder what Dylan's doing now?
ASHLEY
I did at first, but I don't anymore.
LANCE
I know what he's doing.
ASHLEY
Really? And what exactly is it you think he's doing?
LANCE
He's wondering who's kissing you now. At least I would be.

LANCE

I WONDER WHO'S KISSING HER NOW

YOU HAVE LOVED LOTS OF GIRLS IN THE SWEET LONG AGO
AND EACH ONE HAS MEANT HEAVEN TO YOU

YOU HAVE VOWED YOUR AFFECTION TO EACH ONE IN TURN
AND HAVE SWORN TO THEM ALL YOU'D BE TRUE.
YOU HAVE KISSED 'NEATH THE MOON WHILE THE WORLD SEEMED IN TUNE
THEN YOU LEFT HER TO HUNT A NEW GAME.
DOES IT EVER OCCUR TO YOU LATER MY BOY
THAT SHE'S PROBABLY DOING THE SAME?

I WONDER WHO'S KISSING HER NOW, I WONDER WHO'S TEACHING HER HOW,
WONDER WHO'S LOOKING INTO HER EYES, BREATHING SIGHS, TELLING LIES.
I WONDER WHO'S BUYING THE WINE FOR LIPS THAT I USED TO CALL MINE.
I WONDER IF SHE EVER TELLS HIM OF ME, I WONDER WHO'S KISSING HER NOW.

(MUSICAL INTERLUDE FOR DANCING.)

I WONDER WHO'S KISSING HER NOW, I WONDER WHO'S TEACHING HER HOW,
WONDER WHO'S LOOKING INTO HER EYES, BREATHING SIGHS, TELLING LIES.
I WONDER WHO'S BUYING THE WINE FOR LIPS THAT I USED TO CALL MINE.
I WONDER IF SHE EVER TELLS HIM OF ME, I WONDER WHO'S KISSING HER NOW.

ACT 1
Scene 11

The Lady Marmalade. ASHLEY, and SAVANNAH are hanging Christmas garlands, wreaths and lights etc. MISS MARGARET enters.

MISS MARGARET
My house hasn't looked this festive since Hubert and I were newlyweds! And those reviews y'all left on Holler and Trip Advice have gotten the reservations rolling in!
ASHLEY
You just wait until we get The Lady Marmalade website finished with all pictures of the place decked out for Christmas.
SAVANNAH
Yep. We're gonna help close that digital divide for you Miss Margaret. Once we're finished, The Lady Marmalade will be on every internet marketing and social media platform we know of and you'll have more guests than you can imagine.
MISS MARGARET
I can't thank you girls enough. I'm sorry about y'all missing your pageant and missing Christmas with your families but I hope we can salvage a happy holiday for y'all here in Bug Tussle.
SAVANNAH
I'd say it's going pretty darn well for me so far. Stephen sure is nice. We made snow angels earlier today while we were collecting more magnolia leaves (branches, etc.)
ASHLEY
I thought you might have the hots for him.
SAVANNAH
(Sputtering) I don't have the hots for him! He's just nice is all. He's got that Cajun Charisma. I found out he's from New Orleans.
MISS MARGARET
Oh, New Orleans. When I was younger, my girlfriends and I went to Mardis Gras, even though we weren't Catholic and

didn't really understand what was going on. We took a ride on a riverboat, shopped in the French Market, and ate beignets at Cafe Du Monde.
ASHLEY
No beads right?
MISS MARGARET
Oh yes, I forgot about that. We got half naked as jaybirds and got us some beads.
SAVANNAH
Miss Margaret!
MISS MARGARET
I'm kidding, Savannah. Thankfully that wasn't a thing back then.
ASHLEY
I still can't unsee that.
MISS MARGARET
I'd take a quiet night at home with my Hubert any time over those days.
SAVANNAH
What did you and Mr. Hubert used to do for Christmas?
MISS MARGARET
Well, we weren't fortunate enough to have any children but every year we volunteered doing things like cooking a Christmas dinner for the poor, wrapping up toys for needy children, taking meals on wheels, visiting folks in the hospital. We stayed busy.
SAVANNAH
That is so sweet.
MISS MARGARET
It never seemed lonely. Then we'd come back here and sit next to the tree and give each other a few little gifts and listen to Christmas carols..even sing a few.

MISS MARGARET begins to hum Bring a Torch Jeanette Isabella. The music begins and ASHLEY and SAVANNAH sing a beautiful rendition.The girls are continuing to decorate during the song.

ASHLEY, SAVANNAH

BRING A TORCH JEANETTE, ISABELLA

BRING A TORCH, JEANETTE, ISABELLA
BRING A TORCH, COME SWIFTLY AND RUN!
CHRIST IS BORN, TELL THE FOLK OF THE VILLAGE
JESUS IS SLEEPING IN HIS CRADLE
AH! AH! BEAUTIFUL IS THE MOTHER
AH! AH! BEAUTIFUL IS HER SON!
QUIET NOW WHILE THE CHILD IS SLEEPING
IT IS WRONG TO TALK SO LOUD
SILENCE NOW, AS WE GATHER AROUND HIM.
LEST THE SOUND SHOULD AWAKEN JESUS.
HUSH! HUSH! SEE HOW FAST HE SLUMBERS!
HUSH! HUSH! SEE HOW FAST HE SLEEPS!
HASTEN NOW, GOOD FOLK OF THE VILLAGE
HASTEN NOW THE CHRIST CHILD TO SEE.
YOU WILL FIND HIM ASLEEP IN THE MANGER
QUIETLY COME AND WHISPER SOFTLY,
HUSH! HUSH! PEACEFULLY NOW HE SLUMBERS.
HUSH! HUSH! PEACEFULLY NOW HE SLEEPS.
HUSH! HUSH! PEACEFULLY NOW HE SLUMBERS.
HUSH! HUSH! PEACEFULLY NOW HE SLEEPS.
HUSH! HUSH! PEACEFULLY NOW HE SLUMBERS.
HUSH! HUSH! PEACEFULLY NOW HE SLEEPS.

  STEPHEN and LANCE enter.

LANCE
We've chopped and stacked enough firewood for you and your guests for practically the rest of the winter.
STEPHEN
If you wouldn't mind, do you think we could borrow the tank tonight?
MISS MARGARET
Of course, you can. If you happen to find yourself near The Waffle Barn, do you think I could get another Kit and

Kaboodle? Once this snow melts, I've got to stock up on proper groceries to feed my guests. I'm afraid y'all caught me a little unprepared.
SAVANNAH
(Overly eager) We'd be happy to!

ACT 1
Scene 12

The Waffle Barn. RUBY SUE is sitting in a booth with a stack of papers and receipts. DEWAYNE is standing by her. HARLEY is wiping down the counter.

DEWAYNE
You know the rules Ruby Sue. The booths are for two or more customers. Singles have to sit at the bar.
RUBY SUE
Dewayne! Can you not see that I am working on something! I need room! And there's nobody else in here for heaven's sake!
DEWAYNE
Rules are rules. I'll move the condiment rack (pastries, etc.) so you can spread out.
RUBY SUE
You'd think you'd be a little more forgiving since it's Ladies' Day at The Waffle Barn.

RUBY SUE starts stuffing her papers and receipts in her bag.

DEWAYNE
Oh, Ruby Sue. Every day is ladies' day with me.

DEWAYNE

DEWAYNE sings this song as he helps Ruby Sue gather her things and escorts her to the counter.

EVERYDAY IS LADIES' DAY WITH ME

I SHOULD LIKE WITHOUT UNDUE REITERATION OF THE EGO, TO EXPLAIN HOW VERY HARD I FIND IT IS TO MAKE MY PAY GO, ROUND AMONG MY VULGAR CREDITORS I'M FEARFULLY IN DEBT, FOR I ALWAYS HAVE AFFORDED ANYTHING THAT I COULD GET! BUT I MUST SAY I'VE ENJOYED THE BEST OF WHAT THERE IS IN LIFE, I'VE BEEN LUCKY IN MY LOVE AFFAIRS I'VE

NEVER HAD A WIFE! I CAN SUMMON LITTLE INT'REST
IN THE DRY AFFAIRS OF STATE, AND THE BUS'NESS
MEN WHO CALL ON ME ARE COLDLY LEFT TO WAIT.

FOR EVERY DAY IS LADIES' DAY WITH ME
I'M QUITE AT THEIR DISPOSAL ALL THE WHILE
AND MY PLEASURE IT IS DOUBLE IF THEY COME TO ME
IN TROUBLE,
FOR I ALWAYS FIND A WAY TO MAKE THEM SMILE, THE
LITTLE DARLINGS!
NO DOUBT I SHOULD HAVE MARRIED LONG AGO!
IT'S THE PROPER THING TO DO YOU'LL ALL AGREE!
BUT I NEVER COULD FIND ANY FUN IN WASTING ALL
MY TIME ON ONE,
OH, EVERYDAY IS LADIES' DAY WITH ME

IT'S A FRIGHTFULL THING TO THINK OF ALL THE
HEARTS THAT I HAVE BROKEN,
ALTHO' EACH ONE FELL IN LOVE WITH ME WITHOUT
THE SLIGHTEST TOKEN,
THAT MY FATAL GIFT OF BEAUTY HAD INFLAMED
THEIR LITTLE HEARTS
BUT I FOUND THAT ONE SMALL FAVOR ALWAYS
SEEMED TO EASE THE SMART
A POSITION FOR HER COUSIN, OR A LOAN TO DEAR
PAPA, JUST A DAINTY DIAMOND NECKLACE OR A FANCY
MOTORCAR
BUT I DON'T BEGRUDGE THOSE LITTLE DEARS
THOSE NECKLACES OR PEARLS,
ALL THE MONEY THAT I'VE EVER SAVED IS WHAT I'VE
SPENT ON GIRLS

FOR, EVERYDAY IS LADIES' DAY WITH ME
I'M QUITE AT THEIR DISPOSAL ALL THE WHILE
AND MY PLEASURE IT IS DOUBLE IF THEY COME TO ME
IN TROUBLE,
FOR I ALWAYS FIND A WAY TO MAKE THEM SMILE, THE
LITTLE DEVILS!
NO DOUBT I SHOULD HAVE MARRIED LONG AGO!

IT'S THE PROPER THING TO DO YOU'LL ALL AGREE!
BUT I NEVER COULD FIND ANY FUN IN WASTING ALL
MY TIME ON ONE,
SO EVERYDAY IS LADIES' DAY WITH ME

(DANCE INTERLUDE)

I'VE NO DOUBT I SHOULD HAVE MARRIED LONG AGO!
IT'S THE PROPER THING TO DO I'LL AGREE!
BUT I NEVER COULD FIND ANY FUN IN WASTING ALL
MY TIME ON ONE,
SO EVERYDAY IS LADIES' DAY WITH ME

STEPHEN, LANCE, SAVANNAH, and ASHLEY enter.

DEWAYNE
Have a seat anywhere you like! (He gives Ruby Sue a look.)

STEPHEN, LANCE, ASHLEY, and SAVANNAH have a seat at a booth.

RUBY SUE
Hmmmph!
SAVANNAH
I just can't believe the entire town is shut down, but you guys are open.

HARLEY approaches the booth with her order pad.

HARLEY
The Waffle Barn is a cruel master.
SAVANNAH
How did you get to work? Don't tell me you have a tank too.
HARLEY
No, I've just got a slave drivin' boss who happens to own a giant truck with four-wheel drive.
DEWAYNE
The Waffle Barn is open come hell or high water. That's our motto. As a matter of fact, FEMA has what they call a WBDI,

The Waffle Barn Disaster Index.
STEPHEN
What?
DEWAYNE
The Waffle Barn Disaster Index. It's one way they rate natural disasters.
LANCE
You've got to be kidding.
DEWAYNE
It's true. If Waffle Barn is open, it's code green. If Waffle Barn goes to a limited menu it's code yellow. And if Waffle Barn is closed FEMA issues a code red and it's go time.
LANCE
Is that true?
HARLEY
It is indeed true. Most Waffle Barns are in the South and since we get hit with the most tornadoes and hurricanes, we have the best risk management and disaster preparedness.
LANCE
Unreal.
DEWAYNE
People in the South are survivors. If we get down, you know it's bad.
ASHLEY
Case in point. We are staying at a bed and breakfast that possesses a tank and enough canned food to last through a nuclear winter.
DEWAYNE
There ya go.

BOBBY LOU enters.

BOBBY LOU
I'm sorry I'm late. A possum got into the attic and had a litter of babies. It sounded like a herd of cattle running around up there.
RUBY SUE
How'd you get them out?

BOBBY LOU
I tossed some fox urine powder up there. She picked up her
younguns and skeedaddled right along.
LANCE
I would love to see just how one harvests urine from a fox.
ASHLEY
I wouldn't.
RUBY SUE
Deeyah Gawd. Well now that you're here, we can sit in a booth
and we won't be breaking Dewayne's sacred two to a booth
rule.
DEWAYNE
I thought y'all couldn't stand each other.
RUBY SUE
We can't, but every Christmas we're forced to have the gift pow
wow.
DEWAYNE
The gift pow wow?

RUBY SUE and BOBBY LOU take their place in one of the
booths.

RUBY SUE
Ever since Bobby Lou gave my Peggy Lee a pair of toe socks for
Christmas, we've had the pow wow.
HARLEY
What was so bad about getting toe socks?
RUBY SUE
My Peggy Lee's middle toes are grown together.
BOBBY LOU
I was horrified. I felt terrible.
RUBY SUE
So now we buy the presents for each of our kids and just
exchange receipts. It's just better that way.
BOBBY LOU
No more ANATOMICAL surprises.

HARLEY delivers the drinks to ASHLEY, SAVANNAH,
LANCE, and STEPHEN.

DEWAYNE
Y'all still have Christmas together even though you can't stand each other?
BOBBY LOU
I don't see why in the world Baby Jesus would have to suffer on his birthday just cause we can't get along.
RUBY SUE
Even we can fake it for one day.

MARLA JEAN enters. She pulls out a gun.

MARLA JEAN
Nobody move! I'm mad! I'm broke! And I'm pregnant!
BOBBY LOU
Nobody move because from personal experience I know that is a lethal combination!
INTERMISSION

ACT 2
Scene 1

The Waffle Barn. Everyone is in the same position as before.

MARLA JEAN
Nobody move! This is a stick up!
ASHLEY
Do people really still say that?
MARLA JEAN
A hold up! Whatever! Don't move!
LANCE
Hey, nobody's going to move. Just calm down.
MARLA JEAN
That's just like a man! Telling a pregnant woman to calm down. If you were about to have another human come out of you like candy from a pinata you wouldn't say calm down!
BOBBY LOU
Mister, I think it'd be best that you not say anything else. I've been pregnant four times and the last thing you want is a lecture from a man.
LANCE
Point taken.
MARLA JEAN
I can pay y'all back as soon as the snow storm is over and I can get back to work. But right now I'm gonna need y'all to hand over some money.
BOBBY LOU
What's your name honey?
MARLA JEAN
Marla Jean.
BOBBY LOU
And what low life scoundrel got you into this predicament?
MARLA JEAN
Billy John Middleton.
BOBBY LOU
And how far along were you when he walked out, shirking his duties as a man?

MARLA JEAN
Two months. I'm glad he's gone. I can take care of this baby by myself.
RUBY SUE
Marla Jean. Why do you need money so bad?
MARLA JEAN
I have one payment left on my layaway at the Discount Baby Boutiquatorium, but the snowstorm has put me out of work for two days and I'm gonna be late with my payment and they're gonna put everything back out on the sales floor. I'm not gonna have any baby clothes, or diapers, or blankets, or anything. I've been paying on that layaway for six months!
RUBY SUE
Honey, how much do you have left to pay it all off?
MARLA JEAN
Thirty-eight dollars and sixty-five cents. I would have had it except for the storm. Now I'm gonna have this baby all by myself and it's gonna have to go naked because I can't make the last payment.
RUBY SUE
Marla Jean. I'm sure that if you put that gun down, we'd all be happy to pitch in and loan you the money to pay off your layaway.
MARLA JEAN
I'm not taking any charity.
LANCE
But I'm pretty sure armed robbery is not the way to go either.
MARLA JEAN
Shut up!
BOBBY LOU
I thought I told you to be quiet mister! The last thing she wants is advice from a man right now.
MARLA JEAN
(to Bobby Lou) I like you.
BOBBY LOU
Desperate times call for desperate measures and when you think you're going to bring home a baby with nothing, that's a desperate feeling. Howard and I were piss poor when we had our first baby.

RUBY SUE
Yes they were.
BOBBY LOU
But now we're finer than frog's hair. Marla Jean, give me the gun and Dewayne will make you a Kit and Kaboodle Platter. I bet that baby's hungry.
MARLA JEAN
Hmm. Well, alright. All I've had to eat the past two days is a few cans of beenie weenies. I got snowed in before I could get my bread and milk.

MARLA JEAN hands her gun to BOBBY LOU and takes a seat at the counter.

DEWAYNE
One Whole Kit and Kaboodle coming up.
MARLA JEAN
This hungry baby and I thank you.

BOBBY LOU walks over to MARLA JEAN and hands her the gun.

BOBBY LOU
Here's your gun back honey.
MARLA JEAN
Thank you Miss...
BOBBY LOU
Bobby Lou Bradshaw.
MARLA JEAN
Thank you, Miss Bobby Lou.
BOBBY LOU
And here's a check for your layaway. That's from Ruby Sue. She's my sister and she's got plenty of money so don't you worry about paying her back.
RUBY SUE
What?!
BOBBY LOU
And it's not charity, it's a baby gift.

HARLEY
Marla Jean, how did you get to The Waffle Barn?
MARLA JEAN
My neighbor has a guard donkey that protects his goats. I don't live too far from here so I put a rope on him and rode him over.
SAVANNAH
A guard donkey?
MARLA JEAN
Oh yeah. Donkeys protect goats and sheep from coyotes. They're real territorial. They'll kick a coyote's butt. Literally.
SAVANNAH
Where is he now?
MARLA JEAN
I tied him to the handicapped parking sign. I hope I don't get a ticket.
SAVANNAH
I'm sure it's fine.
MARLA JEAN
Look at you happy couples all snowed in together. Y'all must be honeymooning at The Lady Marmalade with Miss Margaret. I saw the tank.
ASHLEY
Oh no. Nothing like that. I'm with her and he's with him.
MARLA JEAN
Oh my! I mean, not that there's anything wrong with that. I'm sure Miss Margaret was happy to have y'all. And congratulations on your civil unions or whatever they're calling it these days.
LANCE
Oh no. That's not what she means.
ASHLEY
Don't be bashful Marine.
MARLA JEAN
Y'all are all lucky to have each other.

MARLA JEAN

I AIN'T GOT NOBODY

THERE'S A SAYING GOING ROUND
AND I BEGIN TO THINK IT'S TRUE
IT'S AWFUL HARD TO LOVE SOMEONE
WHEN THEY DON'T CARE BOUT YOU
ONCE I HAD A LOVIN' MAN
AS GOOD AS ANY IN THIS TOWN
BUT NOW I'M SAD AND LONELY
FOR HE'S GONE AND TURNED ME DOWN

NOW I AIN'T GOT NOBODY
AND NOBODY CARES FOR ME
AND I'M SO SAD AND LONELY
WON'T SOMEBODY COME AND TAKE A CHANCE WITH ME?
I'LL SING SWEET LOVE SONGS HONEY,
ALL THE TIME
IF YOU'LL COME AND BE MY SWEET BABY MINE
CAUSE I AIN'T GOT NOBODY
AND NOBODY CARES FOR ME

NOW I AIN'T GOT NOBODY
AND NOBODY CARES FOR ME
AND I'M SO SAD AND LONELY
WON'T SOMEBODY COME AND TAKE A CHANCE WITH ME?
I'LL SING SWEET LOVE SONGS HONEY,
ALL THE TIME
IF YOU'LL COME AND BE MY SWEET BABY MINE
CAUSE I AIN'T GOT NOBODY
AND NOBODY CARES FOR ME

CRAWFORD enters. He has a seat at the counter.

DEWAYNE
Well hello, Reverend. The usual?

CRAWFORD
No Dewayne. I'll take the Whole Kit and Kaboodle today. I've been snowed in at the church and the only thing there was some of Miss Betty Jean Price's Chicken Casserole-
BOBBY LOU
That woman can make a casserole!
CRAWFORD
-left over from Thanksgiving.
BOBBY LOU
Ewe!
CRAWFORD
Exactly! I'm starved.
HARLEY
How'd you get here Reverend? Bobby Lou and Ruby Sue have dueling Hummers, those four came by tank, and Marla Jean hijacked her neighbor's donkey.
CRAWFORD
I trudged through the snow for an hour. Sorry it's not as exciting as hijacking a donkey.
MARLA JEAN
It wasn't really that exciting.

HARLEY takes plates to ASHLEY, LANCE, STEPHEN, and SAVANNAH.

HARLEY
Can I get y'all anything else?
STEPHEN
One Whole Kit and Kaboodle to go please, for Miss Margaret.
HARLEY
Coming up.
SAVANNAH
Well, you guys know a lot about us but we don't know that much about y'all. You know I'm from Mississippi and Ashley's from Abilene, Texas and we know Stephen is from the Big Easy. Where are you from Lance?
LANCE
I'm from Bainbridge, Georgia.

SAVANNAH
You have GOT to be kidding! I won the Swine Time Pageant in Bainbridge a few months ago!
ASHLEY
She sure did. It added a thousand dollars to our graduate school fund.
LANCE
I haven't been since I left for the Marines. I won the greased pig contest when I was younger. First prize was a ham.
ASHLEY
We rode a few rides but we didn't have time to enter the greased pig contest.
SAVANNAH
And to think we could have gotten a whole ham out of it.
LANCE
There are other contests too. Corn shucking, chittlin' eating, syrup making, pig racing, hog calling, and of course the Miss Swine Time Pageant.
STEPHEN
I'm not sure about any pageants but in New Orleans we have the Jazz Festival, Crawdad Festival, King Cake Festival, and the Voo Doo Festival.
SAVANNAH
Oo! I wonder if there's a Miss Voo Doo Pageant?! I'd love to enter that, even if one of us wins Miss Chicken Plucker, and we have all the money for school we need.
STEPHEN
Just promise you'll call me in case I'm in town. I go back home every chance I get. There's no place like New Orleans.
SAVANNAH
So I've heard.

STEPHEN

WAY DOWN YONDER IN NEW ORLEANS

WAY DOWN YONDER IN NEW ORLEANS
IN THE LAND OF THE DREAMY DREAMS

THERE'S A GARDEN OF EDEN, YOU KNOW WHAT I
MEAN? CREOLE BABIES WITH FLASHIN' EYES
SOFTLY WHISPER WITH THEIR TENDER SIGHS
STOP WON'T YOU GIVE YOUR LADY FAIR A LITTLE SMILE
YEAH STOP, YA BET YOUR LIFE YOU'LL LINGER THERE A
LITTLE WHILE
WE'VE GOT HEAVEN RIGHT HERE ON EARTH WITH
THOSE BEAUTIFUL QUEENS
WAY DOWN YONDER IN NEW ORLEANS

(MUSICAL INTERLUDE FOR DANCING)

WAY DOWN YONDER IN NEW ORLEANS IN THE LAND OF
THE DREAMY DREAMS
THERE'S A GARDEN OF EDEN, YOU KNOW WHAT I
MEAN? CREOLE BABIES WITH FLASHIN' EYES
SOFTLY WHISPER WITH THEIR TENDER SIGHS
STOP WON'T YOU GIVE YOUR LADY FAIR A LITTLE SMILE
STOP, YA BET YOUR LIFE YOU'LL LINGER THERE A
LITTLE WHILE
WE'VE GOT HEAVEN RIGHT HERE ON EARTH WITH
THOSE BEAUTIFUL QUEENS
WAY DOWN YONDER IN NEW ORLEANS

MARLA JEAN
So you've been snowed in at the church?
CRAWFORD
I'm afraid so. I thought the snow would melt pretty fast like it usually does but it never did.
MARLA JEAN
I know. When I was young I'd get so excited about snow and getting to make a snowman but then the weatherman would say that stuff about no accumulation because the ground was so warm. And my dreams of making a snowman would just melt away with that snow. I can't even get excited about this snow because I see a big fat snowman every time I look in the mirror.

CRAWFORD
God never made a more beautiful creature than a pregnant woman, my daddy would say, and I believe it.
MARLA JEAN
Really? You believe that?
CRAWFORD
I do. I mean, I guess it could be the fact that your cheeks are just still red from being out in the cold when you were riding the donkey over here, but it looks like you're glowing to me.
MARLA JEAN
Well, thank you.
CRAWFORD
Do you know if it's a boy or a girl?
MARLA JEAN
No. I guess I'm old fashioned. I want to be surprised. Everything I have on layaway is completely neutral. You've never seen so much green and yellow.
CRAWFORD
I think green and yellow are nice. All the latest baby magazines say blue and pink are completely over-done.
MARLA JEAN
Thank you very much. I hope the baby agrees.

HARLEY approaches STEPHEN with a to go box.

HARLEY
Here's your Kit and Kaboodle to go. Y'all have a safe tank ride back to Miss Margaret's. I know she's happy to have y'all, especially here at Christmas. She's been so lonely since Mr. Hubert died.
STEPHEN
We plan on fixing that. Ashley is building her a website for The Lady Marmalade and we've been leaving some pretty glowing reviews on Holler and Trip Advice.
HARLEY
While y'all are at it, put in a good word for The Waffle Barn. We need all the customers we can get.
LANCE
Looks like y'all are doing pretty well at the moment, especially

in a town that's snowed in with all of the roads officially closed.
SAVANNAH
I've got an idea! We'll take a picture on the way out of the donkey tied up in front and leave a review about how people will find a way to get to The Waffle Barn come hell or high water or unpredicted snowstorm.
ASHLEY
Well, why stop at the donkey? We could take a picture of the tank too! If that doesn't convince people that the Waffle Barn is worth the trip, I don't know what will.

LANCE, STEPHEN, SAVANNAH, and ASHLEY exit.

DEWAYNE
(to Marla Jean and Crawford) Here are y'all's Whole Kit and Kaboodle's. Enjoy.
MARLA JEAN
I'm kind of embarrassed that I said I was old fashioned about not knowing if I'm having a boy or a girl.
CRAWFORD
Why? I think it's gonna be a nice surprise for you.
MARLA JEAN
Oh, it will be. I'm an unwed mother, Reverend, not exactly an old-fashioned kind of thing.
CRAWFORD
Mary was an unwed mother.
MARLA JEAN
That's true but I didn't get a visit by an angel to tell me how it happened. Unfortunately, I know exactly how it happened.
CRAWFORD
Well, Jesus said, let he who is without sin cast the first stone. Alright! Do we have any takers?!
DEWAYNE
You certainly won't hear a peep from me.
BOBBY LOU AND RUBY SUE
Nothing from the booth, Reverend!

HARLEY
See Marla Jean. I would say everybody makes mistakes, but I can't, because I bet when you see your little baby smiling up at you, the last thing you'd call it is a mistake.
CRAWFORD
Well said, Harley.

HARLEY

THERE'S A LITTLE BIT OF BAD IN EVERY GOOD GIRL

NOBODY EVER SINGS ABOUT THE BAD GIRLS
BECAUSE THE BAD GIRLS ARE SAD
EVERYBODY I KNOW SINGS ABOUT THE GOOD GIRLS
BECAUSE THE GOOD GIRLS, WELL THEY'RE GLAD
TILL YOU'VE BEEN AROUND ONCE OR TWICE
YOU CAN'T TELL THE NAUGHTY FROM THE NICE

THERE'S A LITTLE BIT OF BAD IN EVERY GOOD LITTLE
GIRL, THEY'RE NOT TO BLAME
MOTHER EVE, SHE WAS VERY VERY GOOD, VERY GOOD
BUT EVEN SHE RAISED CAIN
I KNOW A PREACHER'S DAUGHTER WHO NEVER
ORDERS WATER
SO THERE'S A LITTLE BIT OF BAD IN EVERY GOOD
LITTLE GIRL
THEY'RE ALL THE SAME

THERE'S A LITTLE BIT OF BAD IN EVERY GOOD LITTLE
GIRL THEY'RE NOT TO BLAME
THOUGH THEY SEEM LIKE ANGELS IN A DREAM
THEY'RE SO NAUGHTY JUST THE SAME
THEY READ THAT GOOD BOOK SUNDAY
AND THEN SNAPPY STORIES ON MONDAY
SO THERE'S A LITTLE BIT OF BAD IN EVERY GOOD
LITTLE GIRL
THEY'RE ALL THE SAME

ACT 2
Scene 2

The Lady Marmalade. LANCE and STEPHEN have on their Marilyn Monroe robes. ASHLEY and SAVANNAH have on their Elvis robes. MARGARET enters. She has on her Patti Labelle robe.

MARGARET
Since tonight is Christmas Eve, Eve, I have a surprise for everyone. Hubert and I used to give each other one present to open on Christmas Eve, Eve, not anything expensive, just a small gift.
SAVANNAH
But Miss Margaret we don't have you anything.
MARGARET
You've given me more than you can imagine with your company. I'll always remember my first guests as my favorite guests.

MISS MARGARET hands the first gift to STEPHEN.

MISS MARGARET
Stephen...
STEPHEN
It's ...
MARGARET
It's canned Cajun seafood gumbo! If you're ever stranded away from home, you can have a taste of New Orleans.
STEPHEN
Thank you! I'll pack it next time I'm deployed.... and starving.

MISS MARGARET gives a gift to SAVANNAH.

MISS MARGARET
Savannah...
SAVANNAH
It's canned..

MARGARET
Canned Mississippi Mud Pie. The official pie of Mississippi.
ASHLEY
That makes sense.
SAVANNAH
You can CAN pie?
MARGARET
It is shocking what all you can CAN. I've canned meatloaf, cheese, chicken feet broth, peanuts. Honey if you can put something under enough pressure you can CAN it...It will last practically an eternity.
SAVANNAH
Oh..well thanks a bunch.

MISS MARGARET hands a present to LANCE.

MISS MARGARET
Lance...
LANCE
It's canned...
MARGARET
Vidalia onions and grits. A taste of Georgia.

LANCE is overwhelmed. He stands and flings his arms open for a giant hug for MISS MARGARET.

MISS MARGARET
And last but certainly not least.

MISS MARGARET gives a gift to ASHLEY. She begins to open it.

ASHLEY
Let me guess.. a can of...
MARGARET
Nope. Wrong.
ASHLEY
A JAR of?

MARGARET
Guess again.

ASHLEY finishes opening the gift and lifts up a beautiful ornament of a house.

ASHLEY
It's beautiful!
MARGARET
You made The Lady Marmalade so festive for Christmas. I can't thank you enough. The house hasn't looked this pretty since I lost Hubert. I wanted to give you an ornament from The Lady Marmalade so you won't forget how special you made this Christmas.
ASHLEY
Thank you so much.
MARGARET
Well, I'm gonna turn in. I'm too old to keep up with you young whippersnappers. Maybe the roads will open soon and you all can get home to your families.
ALL
Good night don't let the bed bugs bite, Sweet dreams, etc.
LANCE
I would offer up a toast to Christmas Eve Eve, but all we have left is milk...and bread of course.
STEPHEN
I've kind of gotten used to the nightcap party attire. It's pretty comfortable. I hope someone gets me a robe for Christmas, without the wig.
ASHLEY
I don't want to hear a peep out of you two tomorrow about what we're wearing.
LANCE
Should have joined the Marines. You at least always know what you're wearing.
STEPHEN
I guess it's time to break out the nutcracker and the sugar plum fairy costumes?

LANCE
Now what exactly were those for?
SAVANNAH
The production number. It's when all the contestants come out on the stage together and sing and dance before they pick the top ten. For this pageant we all had to be Toyland characters.
LANCE
And you chose nutcracker out of all the toys up for grabs? Sexy teddy bear, Barbie, sexy gingerbread girl!
SAVANNAH
We don't get to choose. The pageant assigns your costume.
LANCE
That's lame.
ASHLEY
Why couldn't this have been the Coosa County Catfish Queen pageant? At least we could have untied our tales and walked around in dull gray jogging suits.
LANCE
So, let me guess. The production number song is.....I'm just gonna throw this out there.....Toyland?
ASHLEY
Nope!
LANCE
What? It's the Miss Toyland Pageant!
SAVANNAH
But the song Toyland is way too slow for an upbeat production number.
STEPHEN
Couldn't they have done a rap version or something?
SAVANNAH
It's in three quarter time and that would have been like doing a waltz to Who Let the Dogs Out. It's just impossible.
STEPHEN
So what was your production number song?
ASHLEY
Not important.
SAVANNAH
It was-

ASHLEY
Anybody else sleepy?
SAVANNAH
Jolly Old St. Nicholas.
LANCE
Well you know we need to hear it.
STEPHEN
It's Christmas Eve Eve! How could you deny two Marines? Two Marines who can't make it home for Christmas.
LANCE
That would be cold to deny us.
SAVANNAH
They're right, Ashley. It might cheer them up.
ASHLEY
They're not sad! They're just manipulating you.
SAVANNAH
Well, it worked. Get up.
ASHLEY
I can't believe I'm doing this.
LANCE
Really? You were gonna do this dressed as a nutcracker.
ASHLEY
Don't remind me.

ASHLEY/SAVANNAH

JOLLY OLD SAINT NICHOLAS

OO OO OO OO....
JOLLY OLD SAINT NICHOLAS, LEAN YOUR EAR THIS WAY, DON'T YOU TELL A SINGLE SOUL WHAT I'M GOING TO SAY.
CHRISTMAS EVE IS COMING SOON,
NOW YOU DEAR OLD MAN,
WHISPER WHAT YOU'LL BRING TO ME, TELL ME IF YOU CAN.

OO OO OO OO

JOLLY OLD SAINT NICHOLAS, LEAN YOUR EAR THIS WAY, DON'T YOU TELL A SINGLE SOUL WHAT I'M GOING TO SAY.
CHRISTMAS EVE IS COMING SOON,
NOW YOU DEAR OLD MAN,
WHISPER WHAT YOU'LL BRING TO ME, TELL ME IF YOU CAN.

LANCE and STEPHEN hop up and begin to mimic the dance. SAVANNAH and ASHLEY exit in a huff.

LANCE/STEPHEN

TELL ME, TELL ME, TELL ME IF YOU CAN
TELL ME, TELL ME, TELL ME IF YOU CAN
TELL ME, TELL ME, TELL ME IF YOU CAN
TELL ME, TELL ME, TELL ME IF YOU CAN

ACT 2
Scene 3

The next morning. The Lady Marmalade. LANCE and STEPHEN are already seated. SAVANNAH and ASHLEY enter. Savannah has on a sugar plum fairy costume and Ashley is clad as a nutcracker.

STEPHEN
We just got a call from the airline. It looks like flights will resume tonight as long as you can get to the airport. The main streets in Spartanburg are supposed to be clear this afternoon. But rural areas are a different story.

SAVANNAH
It's a good thing we have a tank at our disposal.

LANCE
You just have to promise me you'll tell all the children on the plane y'all just flew in from the North Pole.

ASHLEY
Very funny.

MISS MARGARET enters very upset.

MARGARET
I just can't believe this is happening.

ASHLEY
What's wrong Miss Margaret?

MARGARET
Lettie Mae Jenkins just called and told me that Captain Earl said that the Salvation Army is just brimming with toys from the toy drive but the poor folks can't pick them up because the roads are closed. I can't imagine all those poor children waking up to no presents on Christmas morning.

LANCE
We could use the tank and deliver them. Clearly Ashley and Savannah are dressed for the occasion and ready to go spread Christmas cheer.

MARGARET
That would be so kind but there's another problem. None of the volunteers who wrap the presents can get over to the

Salvation Army. They have to be wrapped and labeled. A lot of the presents are clothes for foster children and they have specific sizes and things like that.
ASHLEY
Well I'm sure Dewayne over at the Waffle Barn would let us use his counter to wrap presents on.
SAVANNAH
I'm sure with a little convincing we could get him to bend on his two to a booth rule while we're there.
MARGARET
You'd actually spend your Christmas Eve wrapping all those toys and taking the tank around to deliver them?
ASHLEY
It's like Lance said. We're already dressed for it. And you wouldn't have to make breakfast this morning. We could just grab something at The Waffle Barn.
MARGARET
Y'all wouldn't mind?
ASHLEY
(Too eager) Not at all!

ACT 2
Scene 4

The Waffle Barn. SAVANNAH and ASHLEY are wrapping toys. LANCE and STEPHEN are labeling each tag and adding ribbon and bows. DEWAYNE and EARLINE are sitting together in a booth. Earline is doing her nails and Dewayne has his feet up reading his phone/tablet.

SAVANNAH
Dewayne, thank you so much for letting us use The Waffle Barn to wrap the toys.
DEWAYNE
No problem. It's still pretty slow here since the roads are still closed. I expect it'll pick up tomorrow if the ice starts to melt, especially after all that hoopla y'all put on the internet. Our Waffle Barn Facebook page got over a hundred likes in the last thirty minutes.
STEPHEN
You're doing a good thing Dewayne.
DEWAYNE
Thanks. I figure I can give up the counter and lift the two to a booth policy for a few hours.
ASHLEY
The toyless children of Bug Tussle thank you I'm sure.

MARLA JEAN enters. She looks confused, unsure of whether to take a seat in one of the booths or not.

DEWAYNE
Go ahead and sit in a booth. The Salvation Army's Toy Campaign has dibbs on the counter today.
MARLA JEAN sits in the booth. EARLINE approaches.

EARLINE
How about a Whole Kit and Kaboodle this morning....on the house? (She looks at Dewayne daring him to say anything.)

MARLA JEAN
That would be wonderful, but not on the house. Word is the ice is supposed to start melting tomorrow. I'll be able to get my paycheck at The World of Food and give you what I owe you.
EARLINE
I won't hear of that.
DEWAYNE
I will.
EARLINE
You hush or your Christmas is gonna be slim pickins if you know what I mean.
MARLA JEAN
My stomach's been hurting all night. It must be gas from all those cans of beenie weenies I've been eating.
EARLINE
The Kit and Kaboodle will fix you right up.
MARLA JEAN
If y'all don't mind my asking. What exactly is it y'all are doing? I like your get ups. They're very festive.
SAVANNAH
We're wrapping presents for Captain Earl over at the Salvation Army. The volunteers couldn't make it in.
LANCE
And as far as what they're wearing, they are performing Toyland later tonight to entertain the troops.
MARLA JEAN
Really? Oh, I'd love to hear it. I mean, it'll probably be the only Christmasy thing I get to hear all day, what with the power still being out at my house. I can't even charge my phone to listen to any Christmas carols tonight.
STEPHEN
I'm sure they'd be happy to do that for you Marla Jean.
LANCE
It would be like a Christmas miracle.
ASHLEY
You will pay for this.
SAVANNAH
Ashley, how could we say no?

STEPHEN
That's the Christmas spirit!
ASHLEY
Ugh! O.K.
SAVANNAH
I don't know the song, but I'll sit here and be the toy since I am dressed up like a doll.
ASHLEY
What?!
MARLA JEAN
Please!
ASHLEY

TOYLAND

TOYLAND, TOYLAND
LITTLE GIRL AND BOY LAND WHILE YOU DWELL
WITHIN IT YOU ARE EVER HAPPY THERE CHILDHOOD'S
JOY LAND MYSTIC MERRY TOYLAND
ONCE YOU PASS ITS BORDERS YOU CAN NE'ER RETURN AGAIN

SAVANNAH takes a wrapped gift to MARLA JEAN.

SAVANNAH
We didn't forget the baby. Merry Christmas.
MARLA JEAN
Thank y'all!

CRAWFORD enters, clearly upset.

CRAWFORD
Well, this is it for me. My last meal as the pastor of The First Hope of the Last Chance Baptist Church. My career as a clergyman is over.
DEWAYNE
That didn't last long.

CRAWFORD looks around unsure of where to sit.

MARLA JEAN
You can sit with me Reverend. I promise I won't eat you although by the looks of me it looks like I might.
CRAWFORD
Thank you, Marla Jean. Earline, I'll take a Whole Kit and Kaboodle. It'll probably be my only meal today. I don't have anything left at my house but olives and yams.
MARLA JEAN
Oo! That sounds good.
DEWAYNE
What's wrong Crawford?
CRAWFORD
I just got a very upsetting phone call. The Bobby Gaylord Singers can't sing at The Food Pantry PaLooza this afternoon. Their flight got canceled.
DEWAYNE
Even if they could get to Spartanburg, they couldn't get to Bug Tussle.
CRAWFORD
With God as my witness I would have found a way.
MARLA JEAN
Ole Man Jones has another donkey.
STEPHEN
I could get them in the tank depending on how many singers we're talking about. The tank would probably be limited to me and a trio.
SAVANNAH
We can't be carting around gospel singers. We've got presents to deliver to children.
CRAWFORD
It doesn't matter. They're stuck in Roanoke. The blizzard just hit up there.
EARLINE
Now what is this thing they're missing?
CRAWFORD
It's the big Food Pantry PaLooza fundraiser. It provides our food pantry with eighty percent of the food we give out every year.

EARLINE
Can't you get someone else to do the Palooza-ing?
CRAWFORD
The Bobby Gaylord singers are a big draw. People come from everywhere to see them.
MARLA JEAN
And these people just sing?
CRAWFORD
Yes. But they have a big following.
MARLA JEAN
I would think at The Food Pantry PaLooza people wouldn't care who was singing the Christmas songs as long as there were songs to be heard.
CRAWFORD
Well, I'm still gonna get fired. I can't sing to save my life, or my job.
MARLA JEAN
She can sing. (Points to Ashley who is wrapping a present. Everyone's head snaps to Ashley.)
CRAWFORD
You can sing?
ASHLEY
Me? No.
MARLA JEAN
You shouldn't really lie on the eve of Jesus' birthday.
ASHLEY
I mean I have sung, before. But Savannah's the real singer. (Everyone's head snaps to her and so on and so on.) She always wins the talent division in the pageants.
CRAWFORD
You sing too?
SAVANNAH
Earline is really the one you want. She was the Miss East Bug Tussle Fair Queen and sang for her talent.
CRAWFORD
Earline is that true?

EARLINE
Dewayne is the resident Waffle Barn singer. He's who you need. They probably wouldn't know the difference between Dewayne and Bobby Gaylord.
DEWAYNE
Those Marines can sing! They were showing off for these girls in here one day. You could pass them off as your Bobby Gaylord singers.
MARLA JEAN
I don't know which one of y'all are gonna step up and sing to save the Food Pantry PaLooza but it's not gonna be me. My water just broke!

ACT 2
Scene 5

The Waffle Barn. LANCE and STEPHEN are packing the last few gifts into a bag. SAVANNAH and ASHLEY are cleaning up wrapping paper, ribbons, etc. DEWAYNE is pacing behind the counter. EARLINE is leaning near a booth. We hear a scream from offstage. CRAWFORD is looking nervously toward a door with a restroom sign.

CRAWFORD
Marla Jean, are you O.K. in there?!
MARLA JEAN
(O.S.) No! Tell Earline I was wrong about the beanie weenies giving me gas. Something's coming out, and it's not gas!
CRAWFORD
When's that ambulance gonna get here?!
EARLINE
They said they'd get here as soon as they could.
CRAWFORD
Y'all are Marines! Don't they teach y'all about emergencies and stuff like this?
STEPHEN
No! They teach us to take lives, not bring them into the world!
SAVANNAH
Don't they teach you this stuff in... in... preaching school?!
MARLA JEAN
(O.S. A loud grunt then a scream) Help me!
EARLINE
Well the only thing left to do at this point is pray. And that means you're on!
CRAWFORD
Our Father...who art-
MARLA JEAN
(O.S.) The baby is coming!
EARLINE
Go in there and pray! Not out here!

CRAWFORD exits into the bathroom.

DEWAYNE
The health department better not make a surprise visit or I'm doomed.
EARLINE
Relax! Customers aren't even making a surprise visit today. They're snowed in and it's Christmas Eve!
MARLA JEAN
(O.S. a huge grunt and a yell) Stop praying and do something!

CRAWFORD enters quickly.

CRAWFORD
Dewayne! I need some towels!
DEWAYNE
Earline get the reverend some towels! Some with stains already on them! Not the new ones!

EARLINE grabs some towels and thrusts them toward CRAWFORD.

CRAWFORD
I'm going back in!

CRAWFORD exits into the bathroom.

MARLA JEAN
(O.S.) AAaaaaaaaghhhh!
CRAWFORD
There's a head! Just a head!
EARLINE
The miracle of birth.

CRAWFORD enters.

EARLINE
What are you doing?!
CRAWFORD
It's like a freakshow in there. I can't go back.

MARLA JEAN
(O.S.) Crawford! I need you!
CRAWFORD
Isaiah Forty Thirty One! They will walk and not be faint!

CRAWFORD exits into the bathroom.

MARLA JEAN
(O.S. A huge scream)

CRAWFORD
It's a girl!

Everyone begins to clap and yell and hug.

ALL
A girl/A sweet baby girl!/Thank goodness!

MARLA JEAN enters slowly holding a baby wrapped in dish towels. CRAWFORD enters with his hair standing on end, tie askew, etc. Earline, Samantha, and Ashley swarm Marla Jean to get a look at the baby. The men shake Crawford's hand congratulating him.

MARLA JEAN
I'll bring back the dishtowels Dewayne.
DEWAYNE
Consider them a baby gift.
EARLINE
The ambulance is pulling in!
MARLA JEAN
(to Crawford)
Will you ride in the ambulance with me?
CRAWFORD
Absolutely.
MARLA JEAN
Wait! What about the donkey?!

EARLINE
You don't worry about the donkey. I'll ride him back to ole man Jones's. It won't be my first rodeo on a donkey.
MARLA JEAN
Thank you, Earline!

MARLA JEAN and CRAWFORD exit.

DEWAYNE
I could follow you in the truck.
EARLINE
That'd be good. I haven't been on a donkey since I used to hijack one myself to sneak to Billy Ray's house when we were young. God rest his soul.
DEWAYNE
I could just load the donkey up and we could drive him home.
EARLINE
That sounds like a much better plan. My butt started hurting just thinking about it.
DEWAYNE
Let's go.

DEWAYNE and EARLINE exit. STEPHEN puts on a Santa hat.

STEPHEN
You guys ready to play Santa Claus? Or should I say elves?
SAVANNAH
How exactly did you get to be Santa Claus?
LANCE
We flipped a coin. He lost. He may get to be Santa Claus and hand out the presents, but I get to drive the tank! (Puts on an elf hat, happily)

SAVANNAH and STEPHEN exit. LANCE heads out but notices that ASHLEY isn't moving. She's surveying the Waffle Barn.

LANCE
Aren't you coming?

ASHLEY
I'll be there in just a minute. I think this might be the best Christmas of my life.
LANCE
I'm certainly glad to hear it. And I hope we have many more.

LANCE exits.

ASHLEY

O HOLY NIGHT

O HOLY NIGHT!
THE STARS ARE BRIGHTLY SHINING
IT IS THE NIGHT OF THE DEAR SAVIOR'S BIRTH! LONG LAY THE WORLD IN SIN AND ERROR PINING TILL HE APPEAR'D AND THE SOUL FELT ITS WORTH. A THRILL OF HOPE THE WEARY SOUL REJOICES
FOR YONDER BREAKS A NEW AND GLORIOUS MORN!
FALL ON YOUR KNEES
OH HEAR THE ANGEL VOICES OH NIGHT DIVINE
OH NIGHT WHEN CHRIST WAS BORN OH NIGHT DIVINE
OH NIGHT DIVINE

TRULY HE TAUGHT US TO LOVE ONE ANOTHER HIS LAW IS LOVE AND HIS GOSPEL IS PEACE
CHAINS SHALL HE BREAK FOR THE SLAVE IS OUR BROTHER AND IN HIS NAME ALL OPPRESSION SHALL CEASE
SWEET HYMNS OF JOY IN GRATEFUL CHORUS RAISE WE, LET ALL WITHIN US PRAISE HIS HOLY NAME
FALL ON YOUR KNEES
OH HEAR THE ANGEL VOICES OH NIGHT DIVINE
OH NIGHT WHEN CHRIST WAS BORN OH NIGHT DIVINE
OH NIGHT DIVINE

ACT 2
Scene 6

A Food Pantry PaLooza Sign. CRAWFORD enters.

CRAWFORD
We have one more performance tonight for this year's Food Pantry PaLooza Extravaganza. I want to thank you for coming out to The First Hope of The Last Chance Baptist Church and supporting this great mission for our community. So without further ado, the Food Pantry Palooza Finale!

EARLINE
GO TELL IT ON THE MOUNTAIN OVER THE HILLS AND EVERYWHERE
GO TELL IT ON THE MOUNTAIN THAT JESUS CHRIST IS BORN

SAVANNAH
WHILE SHEPHERDS KEPT THEIR WATCHING O'ER SILENT FLOCKS BY NIGHT
BEHOLD THROUGHOUT THE HEAVENS THERE SHOWN A HOLY LIGHT

ALL
GO TELL IT ON THE MOUNTAIN OVER THE HILLS AND EVERYWHERE
GO TELL IT ON THE MOUNTAIN THAT JESUS CHRIST IS BORN

ASHLEY
THE SHEPHERDS FEARED AND TREMBLED WHEN LOW ABOVE THE EARTH
RANG OUT THE ANGEL CHORUS THAT HAILED OUR SAVIOUR'S BIRTH

ALL
GO TELL IT ON THE MOUNTAIN OVER THE HILLS AND EVERYWHERE

GO TELL IT ON THE MOUNTAIN THAT JESUS CHRIST IS BORN

(THE COMPANY SINGS IN A HAND CLAPPING ROLLICKING ENDING TO THE SONG WHILE EARLINE SINGS OUT FRONT.)

GO TELL IT ON THE MOUNTAIN OVER THE HILLS AND EVERYWHERE
GO TELL IT ON THE MOUNTAIN THAT JESUS CHRIST IS BORN
GO TELL IT

GO TELL IT
GO TELL EVERYBODY
GO TELL IT ON THE MOUNTAIN THAT JESUS CHRIST IS BORN
GO TELL IT ON THE MOUNTAIN
TELL IT OVER THE HILLS AND EVERYWHERE

GO TELL IT ON THE MOUNTAIN
THAT JESUS CHRIST IS BORN

THE END

Props
Welcome to the Spartanburg Airport sign
Two ladies' over night bags
Two large duffel bugs
Wine glasses
Beers
Bottle of wine
Mason Jars
Loaves of Bread
Jugs of milk
Small boombox
Low table centerpiece
Plates
Cups
Spatula
Spoons
Aprons (Miss Margaret/waitresses)
Prop Gun
Dish rags/Dish towels
Napkins
Cell phones (2)
Natural Christmas decorations (wreaths, garlands, pinecones)
Stack of receipts
Check
To go boxes
Wrapped Christmas ornament
3 Bagged/Wrapped Mason Jars
Gift Wrap/Bags/Boxes
Wrapped presents (a special one for Marla Jean)
Elf Hat
Santa Hat
The First Hope of The Last Chance Baptist Church Sign
Food Pantry Palooza Sign
Large bag for presents (red preferably)

Costume Plot

Savannah
Pageant gown, White Robe decorated with rhinestones (as in Elvis Eagle costume) and Elvis Wig attached to hood of robe, Christmas Sportswear Division Costume (from pageant) such as sexy snowman, Christmas tree, sexy elf, etc., sexy Sugar Plum Fairy costume

Ashley
Pageant gown, White Robe decorated with rhinestones (as in Elvis Eagle costume) and Elvis Wig attached to hood of robe, Christmas Sportswear Division Costume (from pageant) such as sexy snowman, Christmas tree, sexy elf, etc., sexy Nutcracker costume

Miss Margaret
Outfits indicative of an older woman, Novelty Christmas aprons, warm hat and gloves, Robe decorated with boas/sequins/rhinestones with a hood that has an afro wig sewn to the top (a la Patti Labelle,) church dress

Dewayne
White cook's shirt, khaki pants, Funny aprons, paper cook's hat, Dress shirt/khakis

Harley
Waitress uniform, church dress, tattoo sleeve

Earline
Waitress uniform, church dress

Lance
Two different long sleeve Marine Corps shirts, jeans or khakis, one dress button down shirt with khaki pants, Robe with a cream Marilyn Monroe "Some Like it Hot" iconic subway dress front sewn to the front of the robe. The robe hood should have a Marilyn Monroe wig sewn to the top.

Stephen
Marine sweatshirt for opening scene with jeans/khakis, two button down or pull over shirts, khaki pants, Robe with a cream Marilyn Monroe "Some Like it Hot" iconic subway dress front sewn to the front of the robe. The robe hood should have a Marilyn Monroe wig sewn to the top.

Bobby Lou
Christmas sweater, jeans, church dress

Ruby Sue
Two very stylish outfits, church dress

Marla Jean
Obnoxious maternity Christmas sweater, jeans, Maternity dress

Crawford
Two dress shirts, khakis

Made in the USA
Columbia, SC
21 August 2024